C004109877 3

D0708123

WARNING!

Scaredy Squirrel insists that everyone put on earmuffs before reading this book.

For Maxime, Marc-Olivier, Thomas, Cédric, Victoria, Simon, Guillaume, Camille, Jérôme, Louis, Maude and Janique

Published by Catnip Books
Catnip Publishing Ltd
14 Greville Street
London
EC1N 8SB

First published in 2011
1 3 5 7 9 10 8 6 4 2

First published in Canada by Kids Can Press Ltd,
25 Dockside Drive, Toronto ON, Canada M5A 0B5

A CIP catalogue for this book is available from the British Library

ISBN 978-1-84647-134-6

The artwork in this book was rendered digitally in Photoshop
The text is set in Potato Cut

Printed in Hong Kong

www.catnippublishing.co.uk

Scaredy Squirrel

has a birthday party

by Melanie Watt

Scaredy Squirrel never has big birthday parties.
He'd rather celebrate alone quietly up in his tree
than party below and risk being taken by surprise.

CALENDAR

A few surprises
Scaredy Squirrel
is afraid could
spoil the party:

clownfish

ants

Bigfoot
confetti
ponies
porcupines

So he plans a small celebration where he's the only life of the party.

BIRTHDAY PARTY CHECKLIST
A) Confirm date of birth
B) Pick a safe location
C) Choose party colours
D) Get tuxedo dry-cleaned
E) Prepare cake recipe
F) Practise breathing (to blow up balloons/blow out candles)
G) Send party invitation to myself
EXHIBIT A
BIRTH CERTIFICATE
This certifies that SCAREDY ORVILLE SQUIRREL
was born on OCTOBER 3RD
at this time 1:28 AND 6 SECONDS in NUT TREE.
Weight 14.8 grams Height 8.24 cm
Cute YES Teeth NO Fleas NO
Left paw print
Right paw print
OFFICIAL IMPORTANT RODENT DOCUMENT
EXHIBIT B
EXHIBIT C

NAME
SCAREDY SQUIRREL
NO.
(PARTY OF 1)
221
221
EXHIBIT D
EXHIBIT E
-NUTTY CAKE RECIPE-
200g flour
220g brown sugar
1 tsp baking soda
1 tsp baking powder
½ tsp salt
1 egg
240ml milk
80ml sunflower oil
480g nuts (120g for non-rodents)
SCAREDY SQUIRREL'S BAKING INSTRUCTIONS:
Preheat oven to 177.8 degrees and keep fire extinguisher nearby.
Verify expiration dates on all ingredients
Mix the dry ingredients then add egg, milk and oil. Do not forget the nuts! Stir clockwise.
Pour carefully into greased pan. Bake for precisely 49 minutes and 32 seconds.
Put on heavy-duty oven gloves and remove from oven.
Let cool and decorate (make it pleasing to the eye).
EXHIBIT F
SCAREDY'S BREATHING CHART
PERFECT
GOOD
OKAY
1 2 3 4 5 6 7 8 9 10 (No. of tries)
EXHIBIT G
Scaredy
YOU'RE INVITED TO SCAREDY SQUIRREL'S BIRTHDAY PARTY!
When? Today at 1:00 p.m.
Where? Nut tree, Unknown Ave.
YES, I CAN
NO, I CAN'T — I HAVE TO WASH MY FUR

Scaredy Squirrel heads
down to post his invitation.
He pauses when he spots a
card tucked inside his mailbox.
ROSES ARE RED,
VIOLETS ARE BLUE,
I JUST HAD TO BE
THE FIRST TO WISH A
HAPPY BIRTHDAY
TO YOU!
Sincerely,
Buddy

Scaredy gives it some thought.
He decides that a kindly gesture
deserves a kindly response.

So he changes the invitation ...

Scaredy 'S BUDDY

YOU'RE INVITED TO
SCAREDY SQUIRREL'S
BIRTHDAY PARTY!

When? Today at 1:00 p.m.
Where? Nut tree, Unknown Ave.

YES, I CAN
NO, I CAN'T — I HAVE TO WASH MY FUR

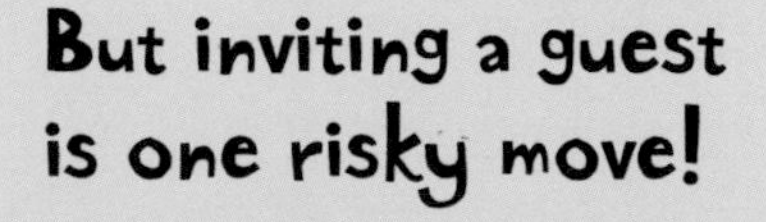

But inviting a guest
is one risky move!

A few last-minute items Scaredy needs to throw a party at ground level:

BIRTHDAY (PARTY OF 2) PLAN
Send invitation to
Buddy on the fly!
Buddy
Party was
up here.
To avoid being
taken for a ride,
attach carrot to
fishing rod to
lure away
ponies.
Party is
moving down
here.
Bigfoot is a huge party crasher!
Build a house of cards so he
stomps on that instead
of the tent.
Confetti gets out of control.
Keep it away by
celebrating under cover!
Clownfish have tricks up
their sleeves and are no
laughing matter!
Humour them with a
hard-headed guest who
will never crack a smile.
Ants are no picnic —
they eat everything in
their path. These party
poopers will hit the road
when they come across
a tasty trail of cookies!
Porcupines and balloons:
need I say more? If disaster pops up,
think fast — put on goggles and earmuffs!
Note to self:
If all else fails, play dead
and cancel the party!
IMPORTANT! The secret to a successful party is all in the details!

DETAIL 1: SELECT CONVERSATION TOPICS FOR SMALL TALK

DETAIL 2: DETERMINE THE DOs AND DON'Ts OF PARTYING

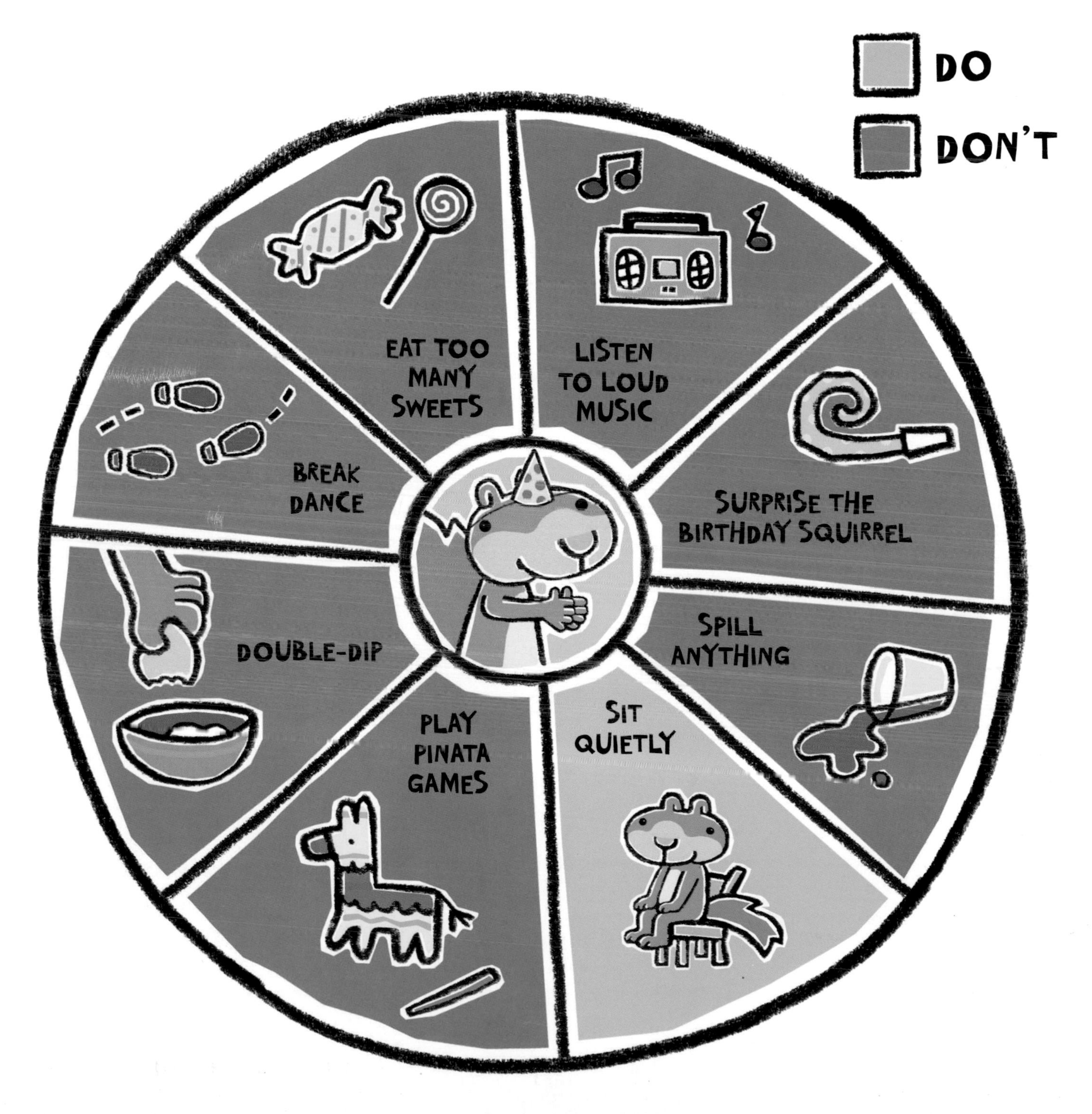

DETAIL 3: PREPARE A BIRTHDAY PARTY SCHEDULE

1:00 p.m.	Serve punch
1:01 p.m.	Look out for:
1:03 p.m.	Serve dip
1:06 p.m.	Brush teeth
1:09 p.m.	Make small talk
1:19 p.m.	Play a quiet game of dominoes
1:24 p.m.	Look out for:
1:26 p.m.	Locate fire extinguisher

1:27 p.m.	Bring out cake 
1:28 p.m.	Take a breath and blow out candle 
1:29 p.m.	Look out for: 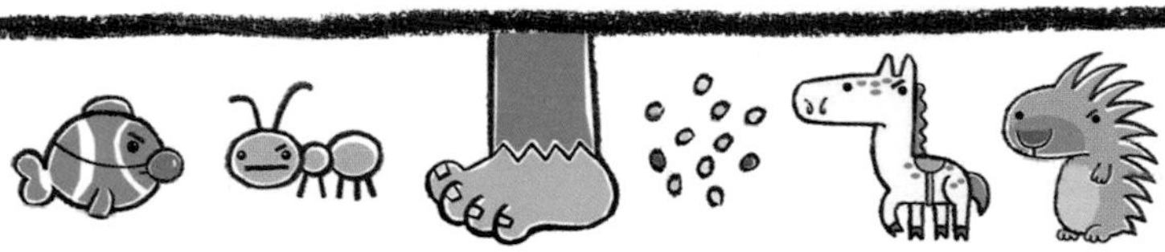
1:31 p.m.	Eat cake 
1:35 p.m.	Brush teeth 
1:38 p.m.	Read thank-you speech 
1:40 p.m.	Look out for: 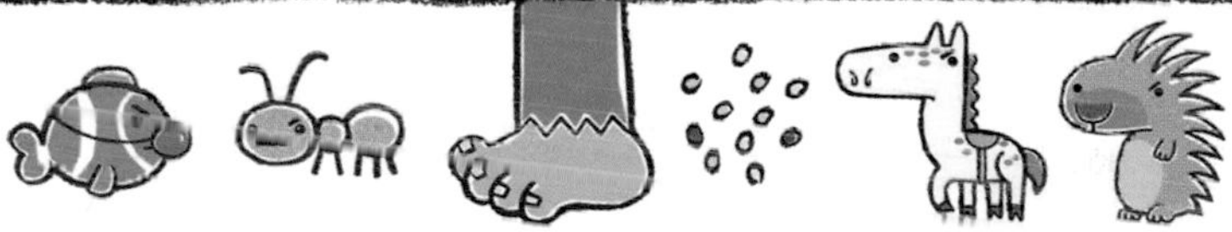
1:42 p.m.	Sit quietly 
2:00 p.m.	The party's over 
2:01 p.m.	Start planning next year's birthday 

HAPPY BIRTHDAY!
CRISPS

Step by step, Scaredy Squirrel carefully prepares for his party. Everything is perfect, right down to the last detail.

But at 1:00 p.m. . . .

Surprise ...
Party animals
appear!

This was
NOT part
of the Plan!

HAPPY BIRTHDAY!
GERM-FREE PARTY
CRISPS
Scaredy Squirrel panics!
He scatters . . .
SIT!
He stops the music . . .

He chases ...
He screams ...
Buddy
He ducks ...
CONFETTI
He freezes and ...

PLAYS DEAD.
seconds later
minutes later
2 hours later

Scaredy Squirrel finally opens his eyes.

He sees that his birthday cake is lit and everyone is sitting quietly.

Scaredy blows out
his birthday candle.
He forgets all about the
clownfish, ants, Bigfoot,
confetti, ponies and
porcupines.

HAPPY BIRTHDAY!

This party is going
to be a piece of cake!

Afterward, Scaredy Squirrel receives something unexpected.

Inside, Scaredy finds a special surprise ...

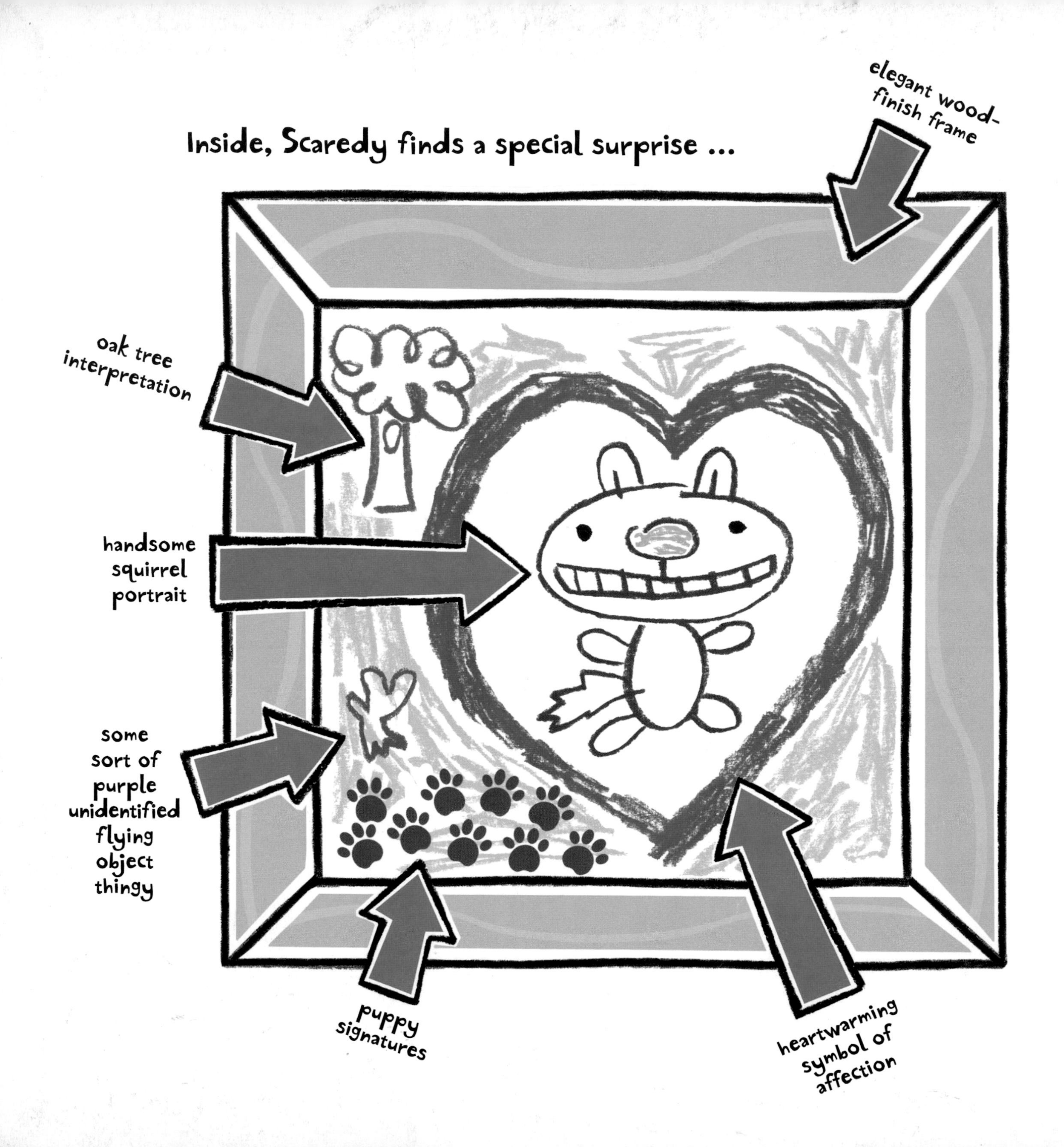

Scaredy gives it some thought. He decides that a kindly gesture deserves a kindly response.

So he changes next year's invitation ...

NEXT YEAR'S BIRTHDAY PARTY CHECKLIST
A) Confirm date of birth
B) Rent larger party tent
C) Choose party colours
D) Dress casual
E) Bake bigger cake
F) Practise breathing to calm down
G) Shrink-wrap everything
H) Buy dog biscuits
NO. (PARTY OF 11)
M) Put on good shoes
N) Wear top-of-the-line earplugs
O) Buy toothbrushes in bulk
P) Get a Frisbee
Q) Install hand-sanitizer dispenser
U) Rent porta-loo
V) Prepare doggy bags
W) Memorize the speech
P.S. This birthday party left Scaredy Squirrel speechless.
thank-you speech